WITHDRAWN
EAST SMITHFIELD LIBRARY
East Smithfield
50 Esmond Street
Esmond, R.I. 02917
401-231-5150

P9-BXZ-516

Leona Devours Books

English edition copyright © 1992 by The Child's World, Inc.
French edition © 1988 by Casterman
All rights reserved. No part of this book may be
reproduced or utilized in any form or by any means
without written permission from the Publisher.
Printed in the United States of America.

Distributed to schools and libraries
in Canada by
SAUNDERS BOOK CO.
Box 308
Collingwood, Ontario, Canada L9Y 3Z7
(800) 461-9120

ISBN 089565-755-4
Library of Congress Cataloging-in-Publication Data
available upon request

Leona

Devours Books

author: Laurence Herbert
illustrator: Frédéric du Bus

The Child's World
Mankato, Minnesota

68,952

Do you like the stories people
tell children? Stories about robbers,
stories about giants, stories about
witches, mystery stories,
funny stories, and stories that are
just plain silly?

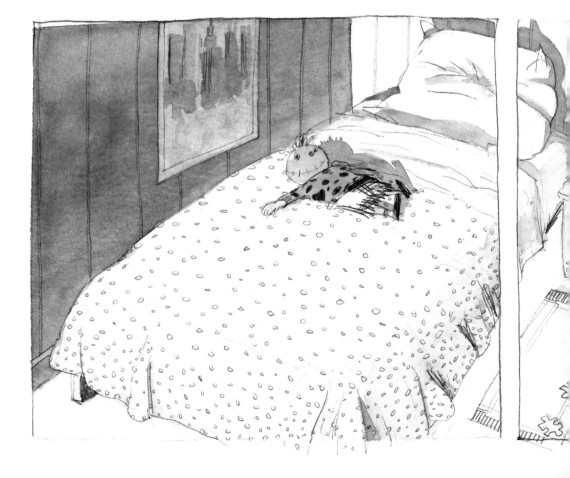

I'm sure you do, but not as much as
Leona does. She likes them so much
that she just gobbles them up.
When I say "gobbles," I know
what I'm talking about. There's not
a single story left on her night table.
You can go see for yourself that
I'm not telling stories this time.

On her birthday we went to the bookstore
and bought her "Little Red Riding Hood."
She liked it so much
she ate it in one mouthful.

As soon as she learned to read, she really took to it and started reading a lot. She devoured with her eyes the stories she liked best. Little by little, things took a more serious turn.

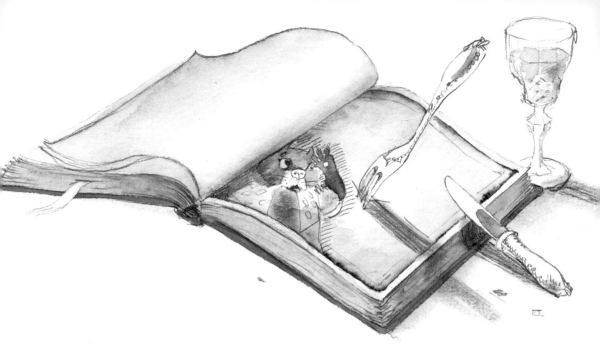

We didn't worry about it at the time.
We pretended not to notice. She did it again. She
swallowed "The Three Little Pigs" whole, and
enjoyed them as much as she had "Cinderella".

Then we thought, "Better watch out,
keep an eye on things, and
see what happens." The next day she ate
"Snow White and the Seven Dwarfs"
in between two slices of bread.
This time we said, "Leona, you really
must not do that!"

But that evening she hid
in the closet and nibbled on
"The Ugly Duckling."
So then we got cross and
shouted "Leona, that's enough!
Eating paper is bad for your health!"

That very minute we made an appointment
with the doctor.

At the doctor's we had to wait an hour. Fortunately, in the waiting room there were some children's books. Without thinking, we started looking through them. While we were busy reading, Leona devoured two or three comic books.

We were quite embarrassed, and when the doctor came to get us, we apologized. He examined Leona from head to foot, and then he told her,

"Stories about kings are bad for your liver, fairy tales are bad for your nose, stories about giants are bad for your teeth, stories about princesses are bad for your back, stories about witches are bad for your whole body."

Leona was good at responding. She said,
"And stories about doctors make you
want to throw up." The doctor had never
come across that illness.

"That's a very rare disease and a quite
peculiar one. I'm sending you to
Professor Knowall — his specialty
is weird illnesses."

Professor Knowall was very smart.

He scratched his head,

then he asked questions.

"Do you prefer sweet stories or scary ones?

Crunchy or soft?

Marinated or browned on top?

With bacon bits or with mushrooms?"

Leona interrupted him,

"Me, I like my stories raw."

Then he said, "Nothing unusual about that.

I get through quite a few myself.

Know what I like best?

I like long stories that put you to sleep.

But I let them stew gently for awhile.

I find it improves the taste."

We thought to ourselves,

"He must be completely crazy!"

We grabbed Leona by the hand

and ran away like rabbits.

We had seen two doctors, and we still hadn't learned anything about the strange disease Leona had accidentally picked up.

So we thought, and thought, then we told some friends about it, and they said, "Maybe Leona's brain is where her stomach ought to be, and her stomach is where her brain should be."

That hadn't occurred to us before. Maybe they were right. Sometimes your stomach sinks into your feet, so why couldn't your stomach be in your head once in awhile?

So we made a decision. No more books in the house!

Leona was no dummy. She went to the library.

She settled in there like in a restaurant

and feasted. "Mother Goose Tales,"

"Jack and the Beanstalk,"

"Tales from the Past" and

"The Seven-League Books."

She devoured them all!

Would you believe that swallowing
all those stories made her think
they were true. By the time she got home,
she was sure she was Cinderella.
She dressed up in an old apron and told us,

"I'm going to clean everything."
No sooner said than done.
She whisked away the dust,
mopped the floors,
cleaned the windows,
washed the curtains,
scrubbed the pans,
put away the dishes,
shook the rugs,
swept under the beds, and
ran the vacuum cleaner for hours.

She scrubbed and polished everything
from the basement to the attic!
We were delighted, of course, and wished
she could always be like this.

The next day she said,
"Today I'm the
Sleeping Beauty.
Good night,
I'm going to sleep
for a hundred years!"
Now that was a nuisance.
We said, "Leona,
stop being foolish!"
But, she fell sound asleep.
We tried everything we could think of
to wake her up. We tickled her,
we shook her, but she kept on sleeping.
She slept for months.

We started to get worried, and tried to think of who could wake her up.

Toward the end of the year we had a good idea. We began asking people if they knew a Prince Charming. Nobody did, so we put an ad in the paper:

WANTED

PRINCE CHARMING

TO WAKE UP SLEEPING BEAUTY.

URGENT!

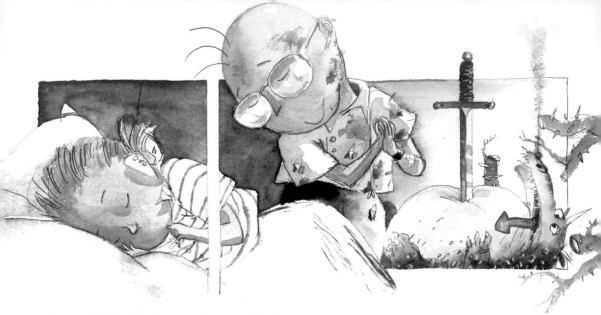

We didn't have to wait long.
The very next day a Prince Charming
came by. He wasn't very big, but he
was absolutely charming, every bit
 as charming as an old-time prince.
He had glasses, a high-pitched voice,
and three hairs on the top of his head.
He went up to Leona and said,

"Sleeping Beauty,
I am Prince Charming.
I am not very tall yet,
and I love chewing gum — I chew it at
recess and when I'm watching TV.
When I'm older I'm going to be a
karate expert and have big muscles.
I'll kiss you if you'll let me."

He gave her a little kiss on the end of her nose, and Leona woke up.

We were quite relieved, and said thank you to Prince Charming for being so helpful.

Before she was hardly awake, Leona asked him if he liked fairy tales.

"I have an attic full of fairy tales!" he exclaimed.

Since they both liked the same things,
they went off together arm-in-arm.

Now as you know, when you marry Prince Charming
you always have a lot of children.
Can you believe it,
Leona had two hundred!

Unfortunately, Leona's
strange illness was hereditary.
Children are often like their mothers.

So to feed them all,
Leona started writing stories.
She wrote stories about robbers,
stories about giants,
stories about witches,
and mystery stories.
She wrote funny stories and stories
that are just plain silly.

THE CHILD'S WORLD LIBRARY

A DAY AT HOME

A PAL FOR MARTIN

APARTMENT FOR RENT

CHARLOTTE AND LEO

THE CHILLY BEAR

THE CRYING CAT

THE HEN WITH THE WOODEN LEG

IF SOPHIE

JOURNEY IN A SHELL

KRUSTNKRUM!

THE LAZY BEAVER

LEONA DEVOURS BOOKS

THE LOVE AFFAIR OF MR. DING AND MRS. DONG

LULU AND THE ARTIST

THE MAGIC SHOES

THE NEXT BALCONY DOWN

OLD MR. BENNET'S CARROTS

THE RANGER SMOKES TOO MUCH

RIVER AT RISK

SCATTERBRAIN SAM

THE TALE OF THE KITE

TIM TIDIES UP

TOMORROW WILL BE A NICE DAY

THE TREE POACHERS